Dear Parent:
Your child's love of reading starts here!

Every child learns to read in a different way and at his or her own speed. Some go back and forth between reading levels and read favorite books again and again. Others read through each level in order. You can help your young reader improve and become more confident by encouraging his or her own interests and abilities. From books your child reads with you to the first books he or she reads alone, there are I Can Read Books for every stage of reading:

SHARED READING
Basic language, word repetition, and whimsical illustrations, ideal for sharing with your emergent reader

BEGINNING READING
Short sentences, familiar words, and simple concepts for children eager to read on their own

READING WITH HELP
Engaging stories, longer sentences, and language play for developing readers

READING ALONE
Complex plots, challenging vocabulary, and high-interest topics for the independent reader

ADVANCED READING
Short paragraphs, chapters, and exciting themes for the perfect bridge to chapter books

I Can Read Books have introduced children to the joy of reading since 1957. Featuring award-winning authors and illustrators and a fabulous cast of beloved characters, I Can Read Books set the standard for beginning readers.

A lifetime of discovery begins with the magical words **"I Can Read!"**

Visit www.icanread.com for information
on enriching your child's reading experience.

I Can Read!™

ADVENTURES OF

BATMAN™

BATMAN created by Bob Kane

HARPER

An Imprint of HarperCollinsPublishers

Table of Contents

Dawn of the Dynamic Duo

Page 9

Reptile Rampage

Page 39

Going Ape

Page 69

Batman versus Man-Bat

Page 99

Who Is Clayface?

Page 129

Dawn of the Dynamic Duo

by John Sazaklis
pictures by Steven E. Gordon
colors by Eric A. Gordon

BATMAN created by Bob Kane

BRUCE WAYNE

Bruce is a rich businessman. Orphaned as a child, he trained his body and mind to become Batman, the Caped Crusader.

TIM DRAKE

Tim is in high school. He is smart and athletic. He is also Robin.

TWO-FACE

Former district attorney Harvey Dent lost his mind when half his face was scarred by acid. Now two men trapped in one body, he bases his crimes on the flip of his special coin.

BATMAN

Batman is an expert martial artist, crime fighter, and inventor. He is known as the World's Greatest Detective.

ROBIN

Robin is Batman's partner and sidekick. Together they keep Gotham City safe. Robin is also known as the Boy Wonder.

NIGHTWING

The original Robin, Dick Grayson grew up and became the hero Nightwing. He protects a city near Gotham and sometimes helps Batman.

Gotham City is a dark
and scary place.
One man helps the police
protect the innocent.
He is a silent guardian.
He is Batman.

Batman is really billionaire Bruce Wayne.

He lives in Wayne Manor.

Underneath is Batman's secret hideout,

the Batcave.

This is where the Dark Knight keeps

the tools he needs to battle his foes.

Batman cannot protect the city alone.

He has a sidekick named Robin.

Robin is a skilled crime fighter

and junior detective.

16

Together, Batman and Robin
are the Dynamic Duo!

Robin's real name is Tim Drake.
Tim is a straight-A student
and a star athlete.

Before he became Robin,

Tim took an oath

to be Batman's partner

and to keep his secret safe.

Tim trained for many months.

He had the best teacher in the world . . .

Batman himself!

Tim learned martial arts, gymnastics,

and how to use different weapons.

He also used science to solve crimes.

When Tim was finally ready,

Batman gave Tim his Robin suit.

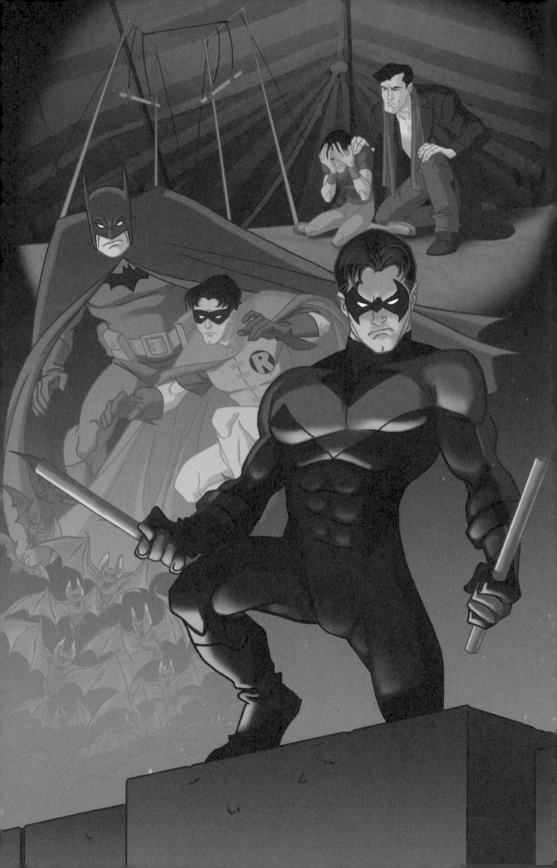

Tim Drake is not the first Robin.

Batman's original sidekick

was a boy named Dick Grayson.

Dick, an orphaned acrobat,

was adopted by Bruce Wayne.

He was also trained to fight crime

as Robin, the Boy Wonder.

When Dick grew older,

he became the hero Nightwing.

Sometimes, he still helps Batman

protect Gotham City.

Bruce and Tim are in the Batcave

when an alarm blares.

There's trouble at the Gotham City Mint.

"It's Two-Face!" Tim yells.

Batman and Robin suit up.

"To the Batmobile!" Batman says.

The heroes zoom into action.

At the mint, Two-Face flips his coin.

"Heads, we steal HALF the cash.

Tails, we steal ALL the cash!"

the crook cackles.

His henchmen are known

as the Two-Ton Gang.

They break into the vault.

As Two-Face reaches for his riches

the Dynamic Duo bursts in.

"Drop the dough!" says Robin.

"Heads up, boys," Two-Face cries.

"It's the bat and the brat!"

After a long fight,

the heroes are overpowered

by the superstrong goons.

"Looks like you're in double trouble,"

Two-Face says to the duo.

The Two-Ton Gang ties up
Batman and Robin.

Each hero is strapped to one side of the
giant penny in the display.

Two-Face has an evil plan.

"Let's break up the set,"

the villain snarls.

"Flip the coin and flatten a foe!"

"Don't be so smug," Batman replies.

"This isn't over yet."

Suddenly, a smoke bomb explodes

and blinds the robbers.

When the smoke clears,

Batman and Robin are free,

and they have a friend by their side.

"Nightwing!" Two-Face cries.

"It's a triple threat!" says Nightwing.

"Get them, you fools!" yells Two-Face.

The Two-Ton Gang rushes at the heroes.

Nightwing helps even out the odds.

He and Robin take on the thugs

as Batman tackles Two-Face.

After a brief battle,

the heroes save the day.

While the police take the crooks to jail,

Batman thanks Nightwing for his help.

"You're lucky I was in the area,"

Nightwing replies with a smile.

"I'm always glad to lend a hand."

Then Nightwing turns to Robin.

"Batman has taught you well.

You two are truly a Dynamic Duo."

Then the visiting hero

disappears into the night.

"We can't rely on luck," Batman says. "We must keep training to stay smarter, stronger, and faster than our foes."

"You're right, Batman," says Robin. "Back to the Batcave!"

Reptile Rampage

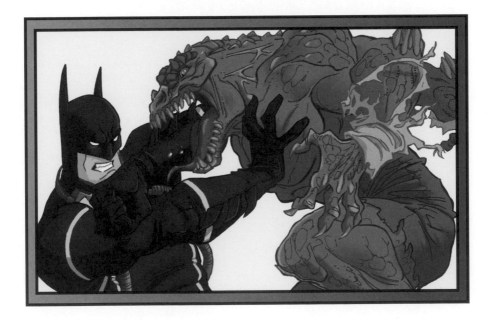

by Katharine Turner

pictures by Steven E. Gordon

colors by Eric A. Gordon

BATMAN created by Bob Kane

BRUCE WAYNE

Bruce is a rich businessman.
He trained his body and mind
to become Batman, the Caped
Crusader.

TIM DRAKE

Tim is in high school.
He is smart and athletic.
He is also Robin.

COMMISSIONER
JAMES GORDON

James W. Gordon is the head of
Gotham's police department and
a close friend of the Dark Knight.

BATMAN

Batman is an expert martial artist, crime fighter, and inventor. He is known as the World's Greatest Detective.

ROBIN

Robin is Batman's partner and sidekick. Together they keep Gotham City safe. Robin is also known as the Boy Wonder.

KILLER CROC

Waylon Jones was once a circus strongman. Now, as a result of a rare skin disease, he is a sewer-dwelling criminal with mutated reptilian features.

Batman is in the Batcave

when he sees the news.

A famous doctor has been kidnapped.

Batman takes the Batmobile

to the doctor's office.

As soon as he sees the evidence,

he knows who is behind this crime.

"Killer Croc," Batman tells the police.

Batman watches a security tape

from the doctor's office.

"Where is the antidote?" Croc yells.

"I don't have it here," the doctor says.

"It's at Gotham General Hospital."

Commissioner Gordon tells
the staff to clear the hospital
while Batman sets his trap.

As night falls over Gotham,

a dark figure sneaks into the hospital.

"This is too easy," Croc says

as he takes the antidote.

But when he turns to leave,

he finds himself face-to-face with Batman.

"Do you have an appointment?"

Batman asks.

"Batman," Croc growls,

"get out of my way."

"I can help you," Batman says.

"The only person who can help me

is me," Croc says.

He charges at the Dark Knight.

Croc is strong, but Batman is fast.

Batman moves out of the way,
and Croc crashes through a window.

Croc lands safely on the street below.

He looks back once

before disappearing into the sewers.

"You let him get away!"

Commissioner Gordon says to Batman.

"No, I didn't," replies Batman.

He holds up a small screen

showing a flashing red dot.

Batman had hidden a tracking device

on Croc's scaly skin.

"He'll take us right to the doctor."

"How will you follow him in the sewers?"

asks the commissioner.

"I can help with that," says a voice.

Robin stands in the doorway.

He is holding two scuba suits.

DANGER

OXYGEN

NO SMOKING - NO OPEN FLAMES

Soon, Batman and Robin are swimming

through the sewers after Croc.

The red dot finally stops moving.

They have found Croc's hideout.

The Dynamic Duo sees

the missing doctor tied up inside.

"I'll untie the doc," Robin whispers.

"You stop the Croc."

Croc is mixing the antidote

he stole so he can cure himself.

"It ends now," Batman says.

Croc whirls around.

"Batman!" Croc says.

"You're just in time for dinner.

My pets are very hungry!"

Suddenly, two crocodiles

swim out of the sewer water.

The crocs are on top of Batman
in an instant.

He reaches for the reptile repellent

in his Utility Belt.

Batman sprays the beasts

and they quickly fall asleep.

Batman catches up to Croc just in time.

"You can't beat me, Batman," Croc cries.

"I'm here to help you," Batman says.

"There are good doctors in prison."

60

"No one's ever helped me before.

Why would they start now?" Croc yells,

and lunges at Batman.

But the Caped Crusader is ready.

The pair wrestles to the ground.
Batman fights to keep himself
out of Croc's jaws.

Robin grabs Croc's antidote.

"You want this, Lizard Lips?" Robin says.

"Come and get it!"

"No!" Croc screams

and dives in after the bottles.

Batman makes sure the doctor is okay before he and Robin dive in after Croc. Croc finds the bottles and then discovers he's not alone.

The Dynamic Duo realizes that they can't beat Croc with strength alone. Batman signals to Robin to split up.

Killer Croc makes a quick choice.

He follows Robin.

He thinks the Boy Wonder

will be easy to catch.

But the Boy Wonder has a plan.

He swims into a narrow pipe.

Croc follows, but he is too big!

Robin climbs out the other side,

but the big beast is stuck.

Later, the police take Killer Croc away to where he can get the help he needs. "Good work, Boy Wonder," Batman says. "That was one tight spot."

BATMAN™

Going Ape

by Laurie S. Sutton
pictures by Steven E. Gordon
colors by Eric A. Gordon

BATMAN created by Bob Kane
SUPERMAN created by Jerry Siegel and Joe Shuster

BRUCE WAYNE

Bruce Wayne is
a very rich man.
He is secretly Batman.

CLARK KENT

Clark Kent is a newspaper
reporter. He is secretly
Superman.

SUPERMAN

Superman has many amazing
powers. He was born on the
planet Krypton.

BATMAN

Batman fights crime in Gotham City. He wears a mask and a cape.

GORILLA GRODD

Gorilla Grodd is a very smart ape. He has the ability to control people's minds.

It was a special day at the Gotham City Zoo.

A new ape exhibit was opening.

All the media was there for the big event.

Clark Kent was covering the story
for the *Daily Planet*.

Bruce Wayne was also there.

He was a guest of honor.

"ROAR!"

Clark and Bruce turned toward the sound.

An ape had gotten out of his cage!

This was no normal animal.

It was Gorilla Grodd!

"Grodd must have let himself be captured to sneak into Gotham," Bruce said.

"We need to stop him," Clark said.

Grodd was very strong and very smart.

He hated humans.

He wanted them to be his slaves.

Grodd had built a special helmet

that he used to control people.

He grabbed a TV cameraman.

"The camera will send my mind waves

to everyone who is watching.

I will take over the world!"

"This is a job for Superman!" Clark said.

"And Batman!" Bruce said.

The two heroes quickly

changed into their costumes.

"Stop this monkey business, Grodd,"
Superman said.

"But I'm just getting started!
I am going to make an army of apes
with my E-Ray," Grodd roared.

Grodd pointed his E-Ray at Batman.

He wanted to make the Caped Crusader

part of his ape army first.

"Batman! Look out!" Superman said.

He jumped in front of his friend.

Superman didn't know

that Grodd had put a kryptonite lens

in the E-ray just for him!

The ray turned Superman into an ape.

"You escaped my E-Ray, Batman,
but you can't get away
from my mind control," Grodd growled.
Batman had a surprise for Grodd.

"My cowl protects me from
mind-control waves," Batman said.
Grodd roared in anger.
"Get him!" Grodd yelled.

In ape form,

Superman was under Grodd's control.

He charged at Batman.

Batman jumped out of the way.

"How can I stop Superman

without hurting him?"

Batman wondered.

While Batman and Superman fought, Grodd made more apes for his army.

"If I want to end this now," Batman said,

"I'm going to need Superman's help."

He moved between Grodd and Superman.

When Superman charged again,

Batman stepped out of the way.

Superman crashed
into Grodd,
sending the E-Ray flying!

Batman grabbed it with his Batrope.

"If I can fix the wiring,

I can reverse the E-Ray,

but I'd better hurry!" Batman said.

Batman quickly fixed the E-Ray

and aimed it at the Man of Steel.

"This will make you feel

more like yourself," Batman said.

With Superman back to normal,

Grodd's mind control was gone.

"I can think for myself again,"

Superman said.

"Enough monkeying around.

Let's cage Grodd."

Superman used his heat vision

to melt Grodd's helmet.

Now Grodd could not control his ape army.

"Get Grodd!" the apes yelled.

The only thing Grodd could do

was run away.

The heroes chased Grodd
into the penguin exhibit.
Grodd slipped on the ice.
Batman lassoed Grodd
with his Batrope.

Then Superman used his freezing breath
to make sure the bad guy could not move.

With the help of the zookeepers,

the police took Grodd away.

And Superman and Batman used the E-Ray

to turn the apes back into people.

Gotham City was safe again.

BATMAN™

Batman versus Man-Bat

by J. E. Bright

pictures by Steven E. Gordon

colors by Eric A. Gordon

BATMAN created by Bob Kane

BATMAN

Batman fights crime in
Gotham City. He wears a
mask and a cape. He is the
World's Greatest Detective.

COMMISSIONER GORDON

James W. Gordon is the
commissioner of the Gotham
City Police Department. He is a
dedicated police detective and
trusted friend of Batman.

MAN-BAT

Before turning into Man-Bat, Dr. Kirk Langstrom was a scientist and an expert on bats. Desperate to stop his growing hearing loss, Langstrom created a special serum that he tested on himself. Instead of curing him, the chemical turned him into a man-sized bat.

It was a moonless night.

Two Gotham City police officers

shouted in shock as a giant bat

landed on their patrol car.

The police officers ran for safety.

One radioed Commissioner Gordon.

"Batman just smashed our car!"

he yelled into his walkie-talkie.

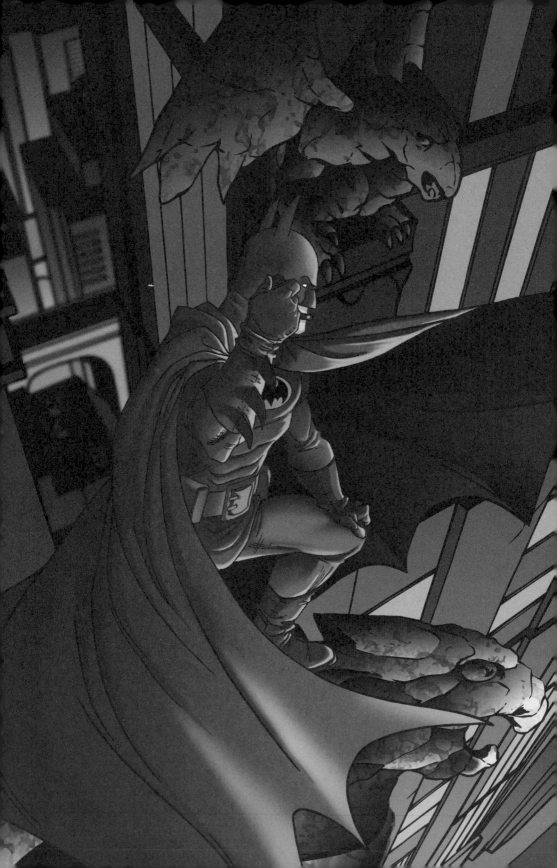

"It wasn't me," said Batman
to Commissioner Gordon.
"I see the creature now."
The strange batlike monster
tore down streetlights
throughout downtown Gotham.

Batman shot his grappling hook.

He caught the creature by the leg.

The giant bat soared into the sky,

dragging Batman with it.

Then the creature bit

through the grappling hook cable.

Batman tumbled onto a roof garden.

The creature escaped into the night.

Bruce Wayne tested the saliva

the creature left on the cable.

It was part human and part bat!

Only one scientist in Gotham

did research on animal hybrids—

Dr. Kirk Langstrom.

Alfred brought Bruce the newspaper.

The headline was BATMAN IS NOW MAN-BAT!

"I have to clear Batman's name,"
growled Bruce.

Dr. Langstrom always worked late, so Batman visited him at night. The Batmobile's headlights showed Man-Bat destroying the lab!

Batman raced to the rescue, leaping through the broken window to save a frightened scientist.

Man-Bat shielded his eyes
from the Batmobile's headlights.
Screaming, he burst out of the lab
through the skylight in the ceiling.

Batman spread his cape

to protect the scientist

from the falling glass.

Batman helped the scientist stand.

"Thank you for saving me," she said.

"I'm Dr. Francine Langstrom,

Kirk's wife and research partner.

That creature . . . is Kirk.

We created a DNA serum

that cured Kirk's deafness,

but it also transformed him

into that angry beast."

"Can you make an antidote?"

asked Batman. "We must save Kirk

and protect Gotham City."

Francine worked all day without stopping.

As the sun set again,

she finally came up with an antidote.

She handed it to Batman and said,

"Be careful.

He's still a human being."

Batman spotted the Bat-Signal and knew

the Commissioner needed his help.

"How can we stop this Man-Bat?"

asked Gordon.

Batman pulled out a tiny sonar device.

"Leave that to me," Batman said.

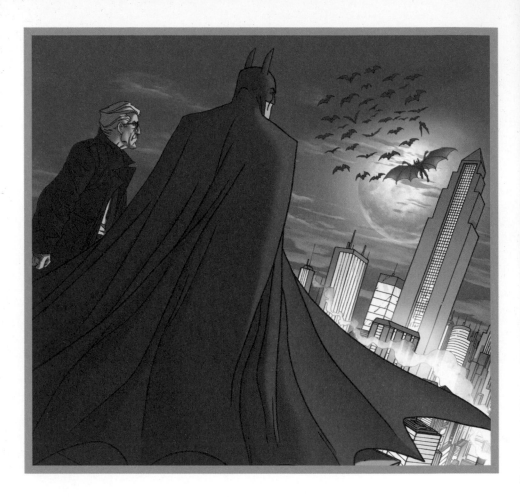

"Kill the Bat-Signal," said Batman.

Bats started to arrive,

called by the sonar device.

"Wait for my command."

Then Man-Bat appeared in the sky.

Man-Bat landed on the roof.

He screeched loudly.

His shriek was painful to Batman's
and Commissioner Gordon's ears.

Hearing the noise,

police officers ran to the roof.

They didn't know Batman was there.

They tried to stop Man-Bat on their own.

Man-Bat easily knocked the police officers
back with his powerful wings.

"My turn," Batman growled. "NOW!"
Commissioner Gordon flashed
the Bat-Signal directly into
Man-Bat's eyes.

Man-Bat screamed in pain

from the bright light in his eyes.

Batman wrestled him to the rooftop,

and gave him the antidote.

The antidote took effect.

Man-Bat stopped struggling.

He looked shocked.

Batman and the police watched
the amazing transformation.
Man-Bat turned back into
Dr. Kirk Langstrom.

Outside the police station,

Francine Langstrom helped

her husband into an ambulance.

The police were taking him

to the hospital for treatment.

"Congratulations, Batman,"

said Commissioner Gordon.

"You've stopped Man-Bat

and cleared your own name."

Batman shook Gordon's hand.

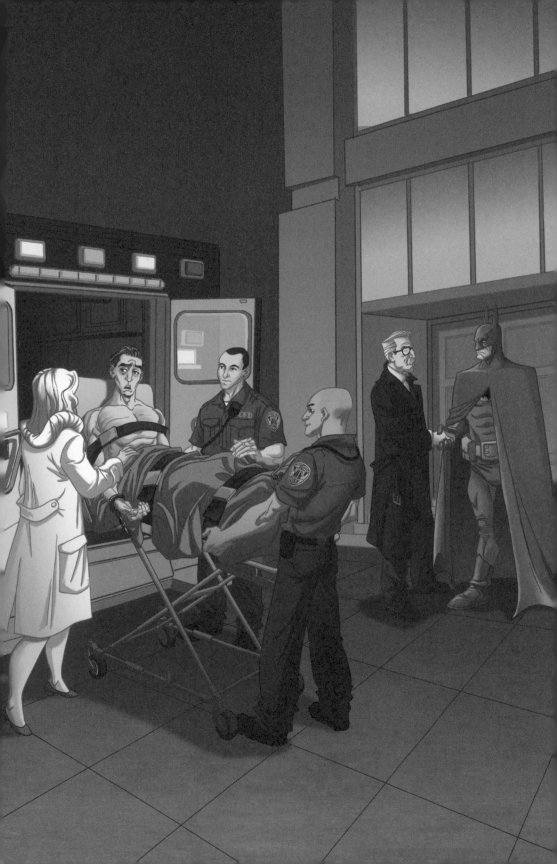

Batman swung home
over the city's rooftops.

"Good-bye, Man-Bat," said Batman.

"Gotham City already has enough
creatures of the night!"

BATMAN ™

Who Is Clayface?

by Donald Lemke

pictures by Steven E. Gordon

colors by Eric A. Gordon

BATMAN created by Bob Kane

BRUCE WAYNE

Bruce is a rich businessman. Orphaned as a child, he trained his body and mind to become Batman, the Caped Crusader.

MATT HAGEN

Matt was a daring treasure hunter. He discovered a mysterious pool of toxic goo, which turned him into the super-villain Clayface.

COMMISSIONER JAMES GORDON

James Gordon is the Gotham City Police Commissioner. He works with Batman to stop crime in the city.

BATMAN

Batman is an expert martial artist, crime fighter, and inventor. He is known as the World's Greatest Detective.

CLAYFACE

Clayface is a shape-shifting villain. His claylike body can mold into any shape or size.

ALFRED PENNYWORTH

Alfred is Bruce Wayne's loyal butler. He knows Bruce is secretly Batman and helps his crime-fighting efforts.

On a stormy afternoon, a man

stepped inside the Gotham City Bank.

He walked toward the front desk,

leaving muddy footprints behind him.

"Welcome, sir," greeted a teller.

"How may I help you today?"

The man smiled.

"I'd like to withdraw some money,"

he said. "One million dollars . . . cash."

The teller counted the man's money

and placed it in a large bag.

Then she handed him some papers.

"Just sign these," the teller said.

The man's hands shook with anger,

and his eyes burned red.

"Don't you know who I am?"

he asked.

Suddenly, his skin started bubbling

and bulging through his suit.

"I'm Bruce Wayne!" the man roared,

fleeing with the bag of cash.

Meanwhile, Batman sped through downtown Gotham in the Batmobile.

The Caped Crusader received a
phone call from his loyal butler.
"Someone's causing a stir
at the bank, sir," said Alfred.
"Who?" asked the masked super hero.
The butler paused for a moment.
"You, Master Wayne," said Alfred,
knowing Batman's secret identity.

Moments later, the Batmobile arrived at the Gotham City Bank. The Dark Knight rushed inside, but the thief was gone.

Then Batman spotted the muddy footprints on the floor. "This crime can be only one man's dirty work," said the World's Greatest Detective.

Batman followed the muddy

footprints back outside the bank.

People crowded the rainy streets,

but the trail led to only one of them.

Batman didn't know the man's face.
However, the Dark Knight knew
he'd found his criminal.
"Clayface!" the super hero shouted
at the evil mud man.

Years earlier, Matt Hagen had been
a young, daring treasure hunter.
While exploring an unknown cave,
he discovered a mysterious pool
filled with radioactive goo.
The toxic jelly changed him
into a powerful shape-shifter.
To maintain this form, Hagen
soon perfected his own toxic goo
and became the villain Clayface!

Clayface fled into the crowd.

"I'll need a bat's-eye view to

catch this crook," said Batman.

The Caped Crusader grabbed a

grapnel gun from his Utility Belt.

He fired the gun's metal hook

at a nearby building.

A super-strong wire

attached to the hook pulled the

hero high above Gotham City.

Soon, Clayface's soft body
weakened in the pouring rain.
Soaring over the city streets,
Batman followed his muddy trail
to shelter in the Gotham Wax Museum.
Dozens of lifelike statues
filled the rundown building.

"Clayface could be any one of these," thought Batman.

"BWAHAHA!" An evil laugh echoed through the exhibit.

Suddenly, the statue of a Spartan
soldier lifted his giant spear.
The villain hurled the weapon
at Batman with all his might.

The Caped Crusader expertly
dodged the spear and then grabbed
a Batarang from his Utility Belt.
"What goes around, comes around,"
he said, tossing the device.

Clayface quickly changed again.
This time, he molded himself into
the Viking warrior Erik the Red!
The mud man blocked the
Batarang with a wooden shield.

The Viking villain laughed.

"You're no match for this blast

from the past," shouted Clayface.

"And soon you'll be history, too!"

"Now, prepare to walk the plank!"
said the mud man, changing into
the evil pirate Blackbeard. "Arrr!"
The villain lunged at Batman
with a sharp sword.

The hero flung another Batarang.
The small, winged device zipped
past the villain's hulking head.
"Missed again!" yelled Clayface.
"But you're getting warmer!"
"That makes two of us," said Batman.

At that moment, the Batarang exploded.

Wooden beams fell around Clayface

and burned like a campfire.

The villain's claylike body quickly

baked into a thick, stony shell.

The Caped Crusader knocked
on Clayface with his gloved fist.
"Looks like you'll be doing some
hard time," said the super hero,
"in Arkham Asylum."

A short while later, the police
arrived at the Gotham Wax Museum.
"That's him," said Batman, pointing
to the exhibit's newest statue.
"Good luck getting him to confess."

Police Commissioner James Gordon

shook Batman's hand.

"Don't worry," he told the hero.

"We'll get this crook to crack." **EXIT**

Batman took to the skies again.

"Now to clean up this money mess
at the bank," said the Dark Knight.

"I don't want the good name of
Bruce Wayne dragged through the mud."